Blue Sky
STUDIOS

THE PEANUTS MOVIE

by SCHULZ

A Friend, Indeed

based on the *Peanuts* comic strip by Charles M. Schulz
adapted by Daphne Pendergrass

Simon Spotlight

New York London Toronto Sydney New Delhi

SIMON SPOTLIGHT

An imprint of Simon & Schuster Children's Publishing Division

1230 Avenue of the Americas, New York, New York 10020

This Simon Spotlight edition September 2015

For information about special discounts for bulk purchases, please contact Simon & Schuster

Special Sales at 1-866-506-1949 or business@simonandschuster.com.

Manufactured in the United States of America 0815 LAK

10 9 8 7 6 5 4 3 2 1

ISBN 978-1-4814-4131-5

ISBN 978-1-4814-4132-2 (eBook)

Charlie Brown is lucky to have a good friend like Linus, a sister like Sally, and a faithful dog like Snoopy. Friendship comes in many shapes and sizes. But what makes a good friend? Charlie Brown is about to find out!

For lots of people, a brother or sister is their very first friend. This is definitely true for Charlie Brown and his sister, Sally.

During Sally's rodeo act in the school talent show, Charlie Brown ran onstage to help her, even though it meant making a fool of himself.

And when Charlie Brown got a perfect score on his standardized test, Sally couldn't wait to show everyone at school all the awesome things about her big brother. She was so proud, she even took kids on a tour of his bedroom!

They say that a dog is "man's best friend," and that's certainly true of Charlie Brown and his faithful dog, Snoopy. Snoopy is the coolest dog in town, and he always has Charlie Brown's back. Whether Charlie Brown needs dancing lessons, an assistant for his magic act, or just a friendly ear, Snoopy is always there to lend a paw!

Friends stand by one another no matter what. After Charlie Brown embarrassed himself at the talent show, a lot of kids in school laughed at him. But his friend Linus didn't care what the other kids thought.

"Don't pay any attention, Charlie Brown," Linus told his friend.

Charlie Brown was happy knowing that Linus was there for him.

THE DOCTOR

Charlie Brown's friend Lucy encourages him too, just in a different way . . . by giving him advice. Sometimes it's hard advice to take (especially when it starts with "You blockhead!"), but at the end of the day, Lucy wants to help her friend succeed.

She even gives Charlie Brown an occasional compliment. "After a lifetime of failures," she once told him, "I have to give you credit for at least showing up."

People become friends for all sorts of reasons. Sometimes it's because they're alike. But sometimes it's because they're different, like Peppermint Patty and Marcie. Peppermint Patty loves playing sports, while Marcie would much prefer to cuddle up in the library with a good book. They might be different, but they balance each other out!

Whenever Peppermint Patty isn't doing well in her schoolwork, Marcie helps her study. And when Marcie needs to relax and have a little fun, Peppermint Patty drags her to the ice rink . . . even if Marcie isn't the most graceful skater!

Friends can be many different things to one another. Snoopy's friend Woodstock is his editor, mechanic, biggest fan, and best supporter. Snoopy's high-flying imagination sometimes gets him in trouble. One time, he imagined he was flying on his doghouse and came in for a hard landing . . . by falling into his water bowl! Woodstock laughed at the sight, which made Snoopy laugh too. That's what friends are for!

But a friend doesn't always have to be another person. Take Linus's blue flannel blanket—he's had it ever since he was little! Just like a good friend, his blanket makes him feel happy and warm, and he takes it everywhere with him—even to school dances!

Schroeder feels about his piano the way Linus feels about his blanket. He wouldn't trade it for anything in the world! He practices every chance he gets, and he even has a keyboard in his school desk. The only person he likes more than his piano is Beethoven, the famous composer whose music he plays!

In the talent show, Schroeder showed off his skill—but it was his love for playing that made him shine onstage.

Schroeder's best friend might be his piano, but Lucy enjoys spending as much time as possible with Schroeder himself! In fact, you can often find Lucy lounging atop Schroeder's piano, telling him about her day while he plays.

And when she was picking her book report partner, Lucy purposely chose Schroeder's name so she could work with him.

"There's no denying it! It was meant to be!" Lucy said, sliding into the seat next to him in class. Schroeder just sighed—he would have rather been book report partners with his piano!

Sally really likes hanging out with Lucy's little brother, Linus. She even has a pet name for him.

"Ahh, my Sweet Babboo!" Sally said as she linked arms with Linus while they were skating. "Isn't he the cutest thing?"

Even though Linus doesn't like the nickname, he just rolled his eyes and kept skating, letting his friend be silly!

Friends don't always show affection the same way though! Peppermint Patty likes teasing her friend Charlie Brown (or "Chuck" as she calls him).

In school, when they went to turn in their tests, their hands touched by mistake.

"Chuck, are you trying to hold my hand, you sly dog?" Peppermint Patty asked loudly so all the kids heard.

Charlie Brown ran out of the classroom, blushing from ear to ear at his friend's joke!

Making new friends can be just as fun as spending time with old ones. In his imagination, Snoopy became fast friends with Fifi, a Parisian poodle with dreams big enough to rival his own. The two pups had lots of things in common, like their love of flying, root beer, and adventures that take them around the world.

From Lucy to Linus to Peppermint Patty, each one of Charlie Brown's pals has taught him about what it means to be a good friend, but when the Little Red-Haired Girl moved to the neighborhood, Charlie Brown felt something different. It was the first time he really wanted to make a new friend.

The Little Red-Haired Girl had moved into the house across the street from Charlie Brown, and they rode the bus together . . . well, sort of: Charlie Brown was too nervous to sit with her, so he hid behind a seat!

When the Little Red-Haired Girl joined Charlie Brown's class later that day, she accidentally dropped her pencil. That was when he noticed something special. "It's got teeth marks—she nibbles her pencils like I do! We have something in common!"

Suddenly Charlie Brown's heart was beating so fast he thought it might burst out of his chest! He went to the nurse's office, thinking he must be sick. But he couldn't stop smiling, and he felt lighter than air. He wasn't sick. . . . He was feeling his first crush!

Still, it wasn't long before all those floaty feelings went away and Charlie Brown just felt nervous!

"You've got to help me, Linus!" Charlie Brown said after school. "Maybe I'm not ready for a serious relationship. How can I support her? I can't afford a mortgage!"

"Charlie Brown, calm down! You haven't even talked to her," Linus said, reminding him to take it one step at a time.

Then with some help from his trusty dog, Charlie Brown finally got up the courage to talk to the Little Red-Haired Girl. The plan was to go to her house across the street, ring the doorbell, and give her a flower.

"I can't believe I'm going to go over and talk to the Little Red-Haired Girl!" Charlie Brown said as he and Snoopy walked to her house.

But when they arrived, Charlie Brown was just too nervous to ring the doorbell.

As time passed, Charlie Brown wanted to meet the Little Red-Haired Girl even more. One night, he saw her dancing in the window of her house! It made him want to find the courage to talk with her, once and for all. . . .

So Charlie Brown went to his friend Lucy for advice.

"Girls want boys who have accomplished things. Do you have a Nobel Peace Prize? A Congressional Medal of Honor?" asked Lucy.

Charlie Brown didn't have any of those things, but he decided to try his best to accomplish something! Snoopy taught Charlie Brown how to dance. Marcie helped Charlie Brown with his book report so he could impress the Little Red-Haired Girl by doing better in school.

Charlie Brown learned a tough lesson: Being yourself is the best way to someone's heart, whether as a friend or something more! Because being good friends—like Snoopy and Woodstock, Marcie and Peppermint Patty, or Charlie Brown and Linus—means liking your friends for everything that makes them who they are!

It turned out Charlie Brown didn't need to be the most talented or smartest kid in school to be liked. After all, his friends liked him already!

The Little Red-Haired Girl saw that Charlie Brown was a good brother to Sally, a good friend to Linus, and a good student who told the truth when he was mistakenly given a high score on a test. It was Charlie Brown's good heart that finally got the Little Red-Haired Girl to notice him!